First U.S. edition 2019
First published by Little Hare Books, an imprint of Hardie Grant Egmont (Australia) 2018

Library of Congress Catalog Card Number pending
ISBN 978-1-5362-0771-2

18 19 20 21 22 23 STF 10 9 8 7 6 5 4 3 2 1

Printed in Shenzhen, Guangdong, China

This book was designed and lettered by David Mackintosh. The illustrations were done in pen, pencil, ink, watercolor, and kraft paper.

Candlewick Press
99 Dover Street
Somerville, Massachusetts 02144

visit us at www.candlewick.com

Waiting for Chicken Smith

David Mackintosh

CANDLEWICK PRESS

For
Fingal Head

I'm waiting for Chicken Smith.

He won't be long now.

Every year, I stay in the same cabin
at the beach with my family, and
every year, Chicken Smith is here with
his dad and his dog, Jelly.

Chicken Smith knows the beach like the
back of his hand, and I do too.

"HEY! LOOK!" my sister calls.

But I'm waiting for Chicken Smith.

He should be here soon.

Every year, Chicken Smith's bike sits on his porch, with his dad's surfboard and the buoy we found in the dunes. Chicken's bedroom window is at the front, and we use it like a door.

Chicken Smith can kick a tennis ball from the top step onto the beach, and Jelly will fetch it every time.

Chicken has carved his initials somewhere around here, and if I can find them, he'll buy me a milkshake.

My sister is calling again, but she'll just have to wait a minute.

Driftwood

Chicken Smith's bike is rusty, with a wheel that rubs on the frame and NO BRAKES. That's OK because Chicken just uses his foot when he wants to slow down.

PROPERTY OF CHICKEN SMITH

My sister yells, "QUICK! LOOK!"

But I'm waiting for Chicken Smith.

She can hang on.

Every year, Chicken Smith and I walk to the lighthouse with sandwiches Chicken's dad makes us. You can still see where Chicken Smith wrote his whole name on the lighthouse door. We hunt for whales through Chicken's binoculars.

Before it gets dark, we race each
other back, in time for dinner.

We swim all day, and sometimes Chicken Smith lets me on his dad's surfboard.

Once, I saw a flying fish, but Chicken says it was either a bird or my imagination.

Last year, Chicken Smith gave me a piece of driftwood he had carved into a whale.
So this year, I got Chicken this crazy shell from the gas-station shop.

My sister likes shells, and things made from shells. She has a collection in a shoebox under her bed.

But shells aren't as good as whales.

For a start, whales can breathe through a hole in the top of their head.

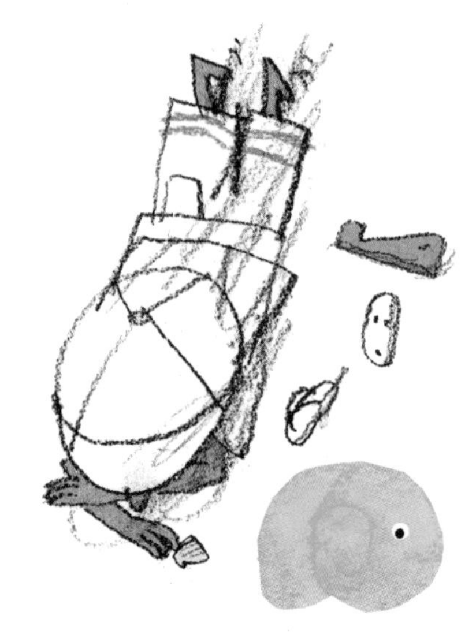

Shells don't.
Shells just sit there
AND SHE STILL LIKES THEM.

Maybe I should have
gotten Chicken
a whale thing
instead?

SIZE: 5
STYLE: BUDGIE
COLOR: TOPAZ

Actually...

if I hold this shell up to my ear,
I can hear the sea — and seagulls squawking.

Now I can hear the ice-cream truck singing — it's a different tune from last year's.

What is taking Chicken Smith so long, anyway? We're missing out on everything.

NO
STANDING
ANY
TIME

This year, Chicken Smith's cabin
looks different.

The windows are shut.
The grass is long, and
I don't see his bike.

Chicken's window has a huge
cobweb with a fly in it.

So I leave the shell there
and walk down to the beach.

Summer
RENTAL
iNQUIRE
AT SHOP

My sister calls again,
but I'm not listening.

"What do you want?"
I call back.

"Just hurry up!"

she yells, running off along the beach.

I follow her . . .

over the dune,
through the trees,
under the pipe where
I once cut my knee,
and up the hill to
the lighthouse.

“LOOK! There he is!”

She points.

And that's the first time I've seen a whale. Even with binoculars, Chicken Smith and I never saw one.

My sister and I watch the whale until our eyes hurt. Then, before it gets dark, I race her back in time for dinner.

At our cabin, we look
at my whale book
until it's late.

Tomorrow we're going
on a shell hunt.

Chicken Smith might
be here next year,
or maybe the one
after that.

I hope so.

And if he's not, I'll give
Mary Ann his crazy shell for
her collection. She'd like that.